Also by Jean Richardson and Dawn Holmes:
Thomas's Minder

First edition for the United States
published 1993 by Barron's Educational Series, Inc.

Text © Copyright 1993 by Jean Richardson
Illustrations © Copyright 1993 by Dawn Holmes

First published 1993 by J. M. Dent, The Orion Publishing
Group, London, England

All inquiries should be addressed to:
Barron's Educational Series, Inc.
250 Wireless Boulevard
Hauppauge, New York 11788

Library of Congress Number: 92-39666
International Standard Book No. 0-8120-5790-2 (hardcover)
0-8120-1553-3 (paperback)

Library of Congress Cataloging-in-Publication Data

Richardson, Jean.
    Out of step/Jean Richardson : illustrated by Dawn Holmes —
1st ed. for the U.S.
        p. cm.
    Summary: Although Rachel outshines her less graceful twin sister
Becky in ballet class, they find that each has a special
contribution to make on the day of their performance.
    ISBN 0-8120-5790-2. — ISBN 0-8120-1553-3 (pbk.)
    [1. Ballet dancing — Fiction. 2. Twins — Fiction. 3. Sisters —
Fiction. 4. Individuality — Fiction] I. Holmes, Dawn, ill.
II. Title.
PZ7.R394850u 1993
[E] — dc20   92-39666
                                                         CIP
                                                          AC

PRINTED IN ITALY
3456   987654321

OUT of STEP

Jean Richardson

Illustrated by
Dawn Holmes

"I'm going to be a ballet dancer when I grow up," said Rachel firmly.

Her sister Rebecca—who liked to be called Becky— looked surprised. She was usually the one who had the ideas.

Because they were identical twins, everyone expected them to be alike—but they weren't. Rachel was as graceful as a swan, and Becky was as clumsy as a baby elephant.

"Perhaps dancing classes will be fun," Becky said doubtfully, "but I think I'd rather be an actress. I'm much better at talking."

But Becky enjoyed the shop crammed with all kinds of dance costumes. She darted around tugging dresses off the racks, and fell in love with the stiff little skirts called *tutus*. When she looked in the mirror, she saw herself floating across the stage on tiptoe....

"You won't be needing skirts like that yet," said the sales clerk. "Beginners need leotards and cardigans, and long socks to keep their leg muscles warm."

"Can I have an orange and purple leotard?" asked Becky, who liked to be different.

"The school says pink or blue with white cardigans," Mom said, hoping Becky wouldn't be difficult.

"Looks nicer with the slippers," added the sales clerk.

Both twins couldn't wait to try on the pink satin ballet shoes.

By the end of the first term, Becky knew she'd never be
a dancer.

Rachel's feet did as they were told. Becky's had a
mind of their own. Rachel's arms made pretty, curving
lines. Becky's drooped like flowers gasping for water.

Rachel danced in time to the music. Becky listened to what the music was saying—and forgot all about keeping time.

As their teacher Mrs. Fishwick said, not meaning to be unkind: "You'd never believe they were twins."

One day Mrs. Fishwick had some exciting news for the class.

"The famous ballerina Natalie Seymour is coming to our end-of-the-year show. She started her training at this school—I remember when she was your age—and we shall have to be on our toes to impress her. Our performance has to be perfect!"

"Can I do…Can I wear…Can we…" Everyone was suddenly talking at once—everyone except Becky. For once, she had nothing to say.

"There's no way I can impress a ballerina," she thought miserably. "If only I could dance like Rachel."

From then on, the class spent all their time rehearsing. Rachel was the wind that danced through the flowers—Becky was one of the flowers.

"I wish I could do something else," said Becky crossly, after Mrs. Fishwick had caught her turning right again when all the other flowers turned left. "Why can't I tell the audience what's happening?"

"We let our feet tell the story," said Mrs. Fishwick, moving Becky into the back row with the boys, who were supposed to be trees.

Rachel felt very sorry for her twin. Becky did try to be graceful, but she waved her branches so eagerly that she nearly hit Rachel in the eye.

As the star of the show, Rachel was to present a bouquet to Natalie Seymour. She was thrilled—until Mrs. Fishwick told her she'd have to make a speech.

"I know I'll get it wrong," she wailed to Becky. "I'm good at dancing, not speaking. I'm good at remembering steps, not words. Can you listen to me again?"

But not this time, the next time, nor the time after, could she get it right.

"I wish I could do it," said Becky, who by now knew Rachel's speech by heart. "I'd much rather make a speech than do that silly dance."

Then the twins looked at each other and had the same idea....

On the great day, Rachel helped Becky pin up her hair and made sure that for once the ribbons of her shoes weren't twisted. When they looked in the mirror, it was hard to tell them apart.

"Let's practice the curtsy again," suggested Rachel. Becky tried to sink down and rise up gracefully, but somehow her feet got tangled up.

"No, like this," said Rachel, but she was laughing so much that she ended up on the floor as well.

There were so many important people waiting to greet
Natalie Seymour that even Becky was a little scared.
She felt a shiver of excitement as a large shiny car drew
up and the photographers raised their cameras.

Flashbulbs flickered on all sides as the ballerina
stepped out of the car and smiled. Becky felt very
small, but very important too.

Now it was her turn to play the star part.

Becky made her speech so beautifully that no one noticed she didn't curtsy. She was enjoying herself so much that she couldn't resist chattering on to Natalie Seymour.

"My sister's going to be a famous dancer like you," she told her, "but I'm hopeless at dancing. Mrs. Fishwick says I've got two left feet."

Natalie Seymour smiled. "Perhaps you're better at talking than dancing," she said.

By now, Mrs. Fishwick had guessed that the chatterbox wasn't Rachel—and it gave her an idea. "Becky dear, why don't you stay with our guest and tell her about our ballet. You're just the right person to explain it."

Rachel, who was waiting in the wings, had no idea what was going on. She'd expected to find Becky with the rest of the class, but when she stole a look at the audience, there she was in the front row, sitting next to Natalie Seymour.

Rachel suddenly realized that she was on her own.

Becky was thinking how glad she was not to be dancing, when she sensed that Rachel needed her. The twins had always been able to read each other's thoughts, especially if they were in trouble. It was as though she could hear Rachel saying, "I want to dance so much, but I'm scared. I can't go on in front of all those people."

Becky shut her eyes, crossed her fingers, and willed Rachel to dance. "It's only stage fright," she told her. "You'll be fine once you start."

But not until she heard the audience clap and someone shout "Brava," did Becky dare to open her eyes.

"What a talented pair you are," said Natalie Seymour, when Becky dragged a shy but triumphant Rachel to meet her. "Becky tells me you want to be a dancer. If you're prepared to work hard, perhaps one day you will be. And I'm sure I haven't heard the last of Becky. On television, perhaps?"

The twins were very proud of each other. Rachel grabbed Becky and whirled her into a dance of joy—and for once both of them knew just the right steps.

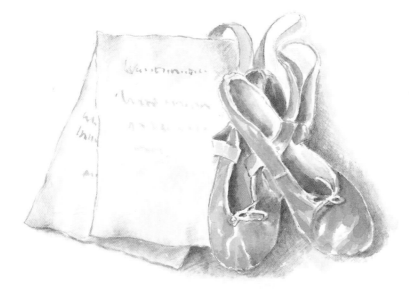